I AM READING

Sniffer's Golden Nose

ROGER ABBOTT

ILLUSTRATED BY

COLIN WEST

KINGFISHER
BOSTON

KINGFISHER
a Houghton Mifflin Company imprint
222 Berkeley Street
Boston, Massachusetts 02116
www.houghtonmifflinbooks.com

First published in 2006
2 4 6 8 10 9 7 5 3 1

Text copyright © Roger Abbott and Colin West 2006
Illustrations copyright © Colin West 2006

The moral right of the author and illustrator has been asserted.

LIBRARY OF CONGRESS CATALOGING-IN-PUBLICATION DATA
has been applied for.

ISBN 0-7534-5959-0
ISBN 978-07534-5959-1

Printed in China
1TR/0106/WKT/SCHOY/115MA/C

Contents

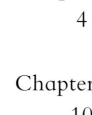

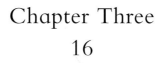

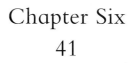

Chapter One

Nancy lived a naughty life deep in
the forest in the land of Trittledore.

Nancy shared her tumbledown cottage
with her pet dog named Sniffer.

Sniffer was a special dog,
a bloodhound, who had a nose
like a ripe, golden tomato.

Naughty Nancy loved all things that glittered. She had trained Sniffer to sniff out anything made out of gold.

Every night Nancy and her bloodhound would sneak off in search of new golden objects.

Nancy would release Sniffer, and he would follow the scent of gold.

Sniffer always returned with something shiny and valuable, which Nancy put inside her sack.

Nancy would carry the new treasures
home to her cottage. Her cupboards
were crammed with golden goodies.

There were golden necklaces, golden candlesticks, golden goblets, golden plates, golden teapots, golden coins, golden rings, golden earrings, golden bracelets, golden brooches, golden trinkets, golden thimbles, and even a golden dog bowl!

Chapter Two

Now, one day in the land of Trittledore, the old king died. His handsome son was declared the new king.

A new crown was made for the occasion.
It was studded with the finest jewels and
made with the shiniest gold.

There were celebrations throughout the land, and everyone admired the new king's splendid treasure.

People could not stop talking about his beautiful new crown, so word spread quickly.

It was not long before Naughty Nancy also heard the news about the king's priceless crown. She became jealous. "I'm going to make that crown my own," she said.

Chapter Three

Naughty Nancy found an old map of
the castle and placed it under Sniffer's
nose to show him where they were
going.

Sniffer gave it several deep sniffs and
wagged his tail. Then they waited
for night to fall.

When the sky had turned black, they crept to the edge of the woods, where they could see the king's castle. Sniffer caught the scent of gold in his nostrils.

Sniffer edged up to the castle and
dived into the moat.

He paddled carefully across the water.

Then he climbed back up the bank
on the other side.

He spied an open window and
scrambled inside the castle.

Sniffer followed the scent of gold.
His muddy paws took him up a flight
of stairs.

He went along a corridor, past the royal bathroom, and into the king's bedroom itself . . .

He carefully picked up the crown in
his mouth and crept out of the room.

Sniffer scampered past some sleeping guards and then paddled back across the moat.

Naughty Nancy was waiting for him at the edge of the forest. She clapped her hands in glee when she saw the golden crown in Sniffer's jaws.

She placed it firmly on her

head and jumped for joy.

The crown really was hers!

Her naughty plan had worked.

So Naughty Nancy danced

all the way home.

Chapter Four

The next morning Naughty Nancy awoke with the crown still on her head. She admired herself in the mirror. "It's so beautiful!" she said with a sigh.

"Now I just need to brush my hair to show off its beauty even more."

Nancy grasped the crown and tried to remove it, but she couldn't. It was stuck. She tugged and tugged and then tugged again even harder, but it just would not budge. "Fiddlesticks!" she cried.

"I need your help, Sniffer," said Nancy.
Sniffer held the crown in his jaws and
pulled hard. But he could not get it off.

"Goose pimples," Nancy muttered.
"What can I try next?"

Nancy wedged the crown in the door
and pulled with all of her strength.
She turned this way and that way,
but it still would not come off.

Just then, Sniffer started barking loudly.
"What's the matter?" Nancy asked.

Naughty Nancy peered through the window to see if anyone was outside. To her horror, she saw the king's soldiers. They were heading toward the cottage.

Chapter Five

Nancy grabbed a towel and wrapped it around her head. She wanted to hide the stolen crown.

Suddenly, there was a loud knock at the door.

Nancy nervously opened the door.

A big soldier stood before her.

"The king's crown has been stolen!"

he snapped.

"We followed some muddy paw prints
from the king's bedroom, which led us
to your house," he added. Nancy's
knees knocked even more.

Then the soldier spotted all of the golden objects in Nancy's cottage. "What a lot of gold you have," he observed.

Sniffer started to sniffle.

Then the soldier spied Nancy's bloodhound. "And what a big nose for a dog!"

Sniffer sniffled even more.

The soldier looked suspicious. "Do you happen to know where the crown is?" he demanded.

Naughty Nancy felt scared and wasn't sure how to reply.

She shook
her head
repeatedly . . .

. . . but as she did
so . . .

. . . the towel
slipped from
her head.

"Aha!" cried the soldier as the crown was revealed. "There it is!"

And so he arrested Nancy and Sniffer on the spot. Nancy knew that there was no escape.

Chapter Six

Naughty Nancy and Sniffer were
taken to the castle and were brought
before the king. Nancy hung her head
low in shame.

The handsome king rose from his throne and stepped toward Nancy.

"Ah, my most precious treasure!" the king said with a sigh. "How lovely, how wonderful, how beautiful!"

But the king was not talking about his crown—he was talking about Nancy.

"I have found my lost treasure," he announced, "and she who wears it I desire even more. Please will you marry me?"

Nancy didn't need to be asked twice.
She nodded her head to accept his
proposal. She liked the idea of
getting married to someone so
handsome and regal.

So, Naughty Nancy stopped being
naughty. She realized what a bad
person she had been. She was truly
sorry and returned all of her stolen things.
But the magnificent crown was forever
stuck on her head.

The king had a new crown made for himself that matched Naughty Nancy's. And they lived together happily ever after.

And as for Sniffer . . . well, he got a job guarding the crown jewels!

About the author and illustrator

Roger Abbott lives in Leicestershire, England, and has been writing short stories since his teens. He conceived

the idea for *Sniffer's Golden Nose* many years ago. Roger says, "As a child, I was always reading and developed a vivid imagination. If Sniffer was my pet dog, I'd certainly be tempted to put his special talent to good use!"

Colin West has been writing and illustrating books for children for as long as he can remember. He works in the attic studio of his house in Epping, England, which he shares with his wife, Cathie. He loves capturing the

right expressions in his drawings of people and had special fun doing the same for Sniffer. Colin says, "I used up nearly all my yellow paint depicting the golden objects in this story!"

Strategies for Independent Readers

Predict

Think about the cover, illustrations, and the title of the book. What do you think this book will be about? While you are reading think about what may happen next and why.

Monitor

As you read ask yourself if what you're reading makes sense. If it doesn't, reread, look at the illustrations, or read ahead.

Question

Ask yourself questions about important ideas in the story such as what the characters might do or what you might learn.

Phonics

If there is a word that you do not know, look carefully at the letters, sounds, and word parts that you do know. Blend the sounds to read the word. Ask yourself if this is a word you know. Does it make sense in the sentence?

Summarize

Think about the characters, the setting where the story takes place, and the problem the characters faced in the story. Tell the important ideas in the beginning, middle, and end of the story.

Evaluate

Ask yourself questions like: Did you like the story? Why or why not? How did the author make the story come alive? How did the author make the story fun to read? How well did you understand the story? Maybe you can understand it better if you read it again!